WHAT IS PASSIVE INCOME

BY

DEEPAK HAJOARY

ISBN 978-93-5438-137-9

© Deepak Hajoary 2020

Published in India 2020 by Pencil

A brand of

One Point Six Technologies Pvt. Ltd.

123, Building J2, Shram Seva Premises,

Wadala Truck Terminal, Wadala (E)

Mumbai 400037, Maharashtra, INDIA

E connect@thepencilapp.com

W www.thepencilapp.com

DISCLAIMER: *The opinions expressed in this book are those of the authors and do not purport to reflect the views of the Publisher.*

Author biography

Deepak Hajoary is engineer by profession. He loves to read and keep himself updated on latest trends. He has desire to learn more and write books on specific genre

Contents

Work From Home Business Opportunity Choices

Work From Home Business Opportunity Choices

You can start a home-based business with little money or no money and with minimal experience. A quick google search will show a huge list of home-based businesses.

When you think of owning and operating a business, you might think about doing things at ease time.

You have the option to pick from numbers upon numbers of home-based commercial enterprises relying on your interest. There are tremendous opportunities to choose, but you have to decide which fits

You have to look through the possibilities and select one of the many that may interest you.

With the rise of home-based businesses, more people tend toward doing business at home.

In today's linked world the place technological know-how affords us greater flexibility in how and the place we work, home-based groups come in a vast range of form

You can be young, old, married, single, have children or only cats and discover a domestic, commercial enterprise that fits your wants and brings you happiness; the preferences are in all places

Home enterprise possibilities can be determined online, in the newspaper, and even although domestic enterprise books from your neighborhood library. Begin searching into these resources, and you will quickly see your self playing your job and excelling in success with an existence full of happiness. A domestic, commercial enterprise probability awaits you to pick out it and make it your own. You need only a room and laptop or computer to start a home-based business.

Who should start a home-based business?

- You should know if it is the right time to start a home-based business. I cannot answer who is the right person to begin to start a business.

- You should do the maths to start a business.

- Ask your instincts

- Decide on factors that motivate you to start a business.

- You should be aware of these considerations:

What kind of business should you choose?

- Staying clear of scams when starting a home-based business

- Buying an existing home-based business or franchise

- Choosing the right entity form for your home-based business

- These question you should answer the above questions. I believe these are not easy but a hard task.

Do you want to be your boss?

- I feel everyone wants to be his boss.

- I don't have the answer to that; you only have to decide what to be done.

Action Plan

Write business Planning

Write a business plan. You should describe the detailed project in writing. It should consist of a simple business strategy about its program. Its short term and long term goal.How it is going to meet the mission and vision.

Research

These days the internet is full of resources. You can find an abundance of funds from the internet. There are lots of databases available to study or get ideas about a specific topic.

You can read articles mentioning specific projects. Do a brainstorming session; the ideas will flow.

Legal Requirement

Is it necessary to register under the government ACT? These legal requirements may vary according to country. Study thoroughly to know about the necessity to start a business. You need to be crystal clear before starting a business.

Business Name

This seems to be simple work. But you can be confusing to set a business name. Well, this seems to be an easy topic, but it may take time to give a proper business name.

Bank Account

You may need to be prepared to share details with your clients. For the business purpose, you have to receive the amount in that account.

Services and Contracts

Do you need services and contracts?

This needs to be clear in doing business. The online store may have to sign a contract between the clients. You have to set a deadline for your services to your customers. Having services and arrangements will make customers clear about the service provider.

Marketing Materials

This is a central part of any business. Well, you need to market your business to aware customers. More the awareness the customers will know the service.

The kind of services offering will reflect on the marketing material. It will be apparent to the customer to know to inquire about the business

Internet Presence

Assume a business without an internet presence.

What will be the condition of the business in the digital world?

In today's digital world, where there is fierce competition, it is an internet presence to gain a competitive advantage.

You have to build a reliable website to make a worldwide presence. Every time the customers see something, theyt\ search at google. Not having an internet presence will be a significant disadvantage to business.

Business Policies

You should have business policies documented. You may see it very easy to do home-based business. There is homework to do. Be the gamechanger and have all the requirements before launching a company.

Steps to Successfully Launch a Home-Based Business

What is your business going to be about?

Who are your customers?

What is your target market?

What are your essential products? What services do you offer?

Who are your competitors?You can figure out all kinds of right answers to fulfill the question bar; however, it is essential to remember your core values and the only one primary purpose that is driving your whole business ahead – it all lies within the word "Why?"

Decide If You Are an Entrepreneur

You have to know the role of an entrepreneur. Once you decide that, make your mindset of that entrepreneur. While running a business, you may face troubles and difficulties. You have to be aware and have the right kind of mindset to operate your company. Positive attitudes and a positive mindset will always help you in functioning a business. Be the boss to answer all the problems. If you format on turning into an entrepreneur, it is integral to exert time and effort in obtaining or bettering the essential competencies for the job. Build Your Business on Your Strengths

The right skills set can help the business to grow faster.

We have to enrich our business skills, Learn from blogs, or take a career class.

If your full-time job and start operating a business, then there may be challenging times .managing times may be difficult. How can a full-time job doer devote ample time for his company? This has to be scheduled or managed time. One has to choose between the two or do a lot of hard work for business.

Write a Business Plan

Write a business plan stating its future goals. The business plan will always guide you in the right direction. If you are distracted, you can always look back. There may come a time for distraction. A clear business plan will have a future goal for the short term and long term.

Find Financing

Do I have money to start a business?

Will my friends lend me the amount?

Will my family help me?

I believe these are some points to think about, but sometime you may not get help from anyone. So always have another plan.

Some online businesses may need less amount. But you need to find a financer to start a business. The opposite is that if you were rich, you might not go for it.

Ask your friends or relatives for support. Finding the source to start a business is the first step in marketing.

Concentrate on your customer

There is a saying customer is the king.

Why do we serve?

Who are my customers?

Are you going to target all segments?

Are you targeting specific segments?

What are my goals?

The first process of any business is to understand the customer's need and wants.you have to have clarity on the needs and demands of consumers. The first step towards customer product is identifying the market segment. You have to understand the specific target market. One has to narrow down the niche to get bright ideas to start. Now, after that, you will be aware of the slot and target segment. Try different ways to find to help the customer. If you deep dive into the process, you will get the necessary base to understand customer demand.

All businesses try to satisfy customers. Customers are significant in the industry. You need to be number one, then serve your customer.the quality of service the customers are provided, then it is likely that they may come back. Customer retention is another factor for any business.

Use the internet

I believe social media is the king these days. Does it matter?

Why do people use social media?

Are you using social media?

Are there any principles to use social media?

Does social media leverage your products?

These are some thoughts on using social media.

The first task is to have a personal website. The name of the website can be your full name and last name. This will build your brand, and people will be more aware of knowing your service offering. Almost all home-based business does have a business website. You can also open a business page on Facebook. Build a Facebook community group and have a business Instagram account. This can create awareness for your business.one has to be super active on social media while having a business page or community group. You can have live sessions with your customers discussing any subject related to business.

You need to have your company on the social platform. You need to explore all possibilities about social media. You may find business people doing business with the help of the page book page. You need to learn to monetize it. The business motive to be explored by customers in almost form. Once your commercial enterprise is on the Web, you are in an international market, so be conscious of language and cultural variations as you submit your content material and ads. Use cheaper advertising techniques to promote your Web

Be prepared

Always be prepared. You cannot be sure that the customer will always like your service. In today's digital world, while there is fierce competition, be ready for the worst.

You cannot say that the problem won't arise. But it will show up at any time.

To learn and grow, you have to be a problem solver.

You never know when the uncertainty will occur. We cannot see the future as it is almost uncertain. To manage possibilities, you need to explore and understand the business.

Have a plan always to meet the future uncertainties and shortfalls. You cannot deny that all business is problems free. Your reason has to be a problem solver, not gainer. No doubt; there will be profit or loss at your business, but tackle customer problems effectively.

Should You Open a Home-Based Business

There can be two sides of a coin. For every business, you can find both advantages and disadvantages. If you ask me the various benefits of starting a simple activity. Then I can write down several points based on that particular topic

Here are some few points :

- Boss

- Enjoy plenty of flexibility

- squeeze more work into your day

- Personal freedom

- Increased opportunity.

- Tax advantages.

- More time for friends and family

- Less stress

- Opportunities for professional growth

- Increased productivity.

- A creative outlet

- Less Stress

- Anyone can start it

- Great income potential

- Personal freedom

- Improved work/life balance

- Personal freedom

Points to stay ahead of the game

1. Workaround the activities –Your clients will apprehend as lengthy as you talk with them. Be truthful that matters may also take a little longer than usual, however, hold your clients up to date as regularly as possible. Communication is the key. Most people will recognize the extend as long as they are conscious of it. If you get to the factor the place, you can't work or can't end a project, however positive to be evident and straightforward about the scenario and strive to make an association that will be acceptable. Also, let them understand as quickly as viable so they can prepare. Don't wait until the remaining minute to propose a functional problem.

   If you are struggling because of a baby being sick, attempt to work when the toddler is sound asleep and do not stress yourself out to work at different times. Make a time table of what desires to be achieved so that you can accomplish as a good deal as viable throughout these times.

2. Don't be afraid to ask for assist –We tend to sense that we must be in a position to deal with the whole thing that is thrown at us. Unfortunately, this simply is not always the case. There are instances when we want

to enable ourselves to ask for help. When a tragedy occurs, and you are honestly overwhelmed, locate any individual who you trust, and ask them for help. Many times, merely having anyone reply to clients on your behalf can take the strain off your shoulders.

3. Prepare for the worst – Because we by no means comprehend what the future holds, it is usually higher to be prepared.

4. Future is uncertain.You should have other plan to adapt to change.

Do the Maths

There ought to continually be solely two sorts of Home Businesses. One is a profitable Home Business, and the difference is a failed Home Business. First, the useful enterprise proprietors have to discover out why the other team failed, and the failed enterprise proprietors must discover out how the different team is successful.

At one specific stage in everyone's life, they will comprehend the significance of time, cash, and freedom. They will research that having a Home commercial enterprise is an asset, and one of the most high-quality structures of enterprise for a person to attain the purpose of having extra time, cash, and freedom.

Home Business Entrepreneurs can be a good source. However, the vital factor is they need to in no way stroll backward. They don't have to worry if their development is sluggish. However, the primary difficulty is, they have to be steady. Slow people, please apprehend that experience makes you modified, Training makes you certified, and solely Involvement makes you blissful and prosperous. If you genuinely desire to experience free time with your family, spend extra cash to fulfill your child's desires, and assist others by using supporting yourselves, then Home Business is the fantastic concept that will help you to reap everything.

Success is no longer an accident. It is the result of your mindset, and your mindset is a choice. Hence success is a be counted of preference and no longer chance. If you prefer to succeed, shape the dependency of doing matters that disasters don't like to do.

Learn the secrets and techniques of success from the existence histories of profitable people. If we become aware of and undertake the qualities, methods, and characteristics of beneficial domestic enterprise owners, you, too, shall be successful. Success in Home Business is no longer magic or underground secrets and techniques to be revealed; it is nothing, however the result of continually making use of some fundamental principles. In-Home Business, success is now not solely incomes million dollars, nonetheless additionally incomes the goodwill of our enterprise associates, purchasers, and followers. Moreover, Success in our Home Business must be duplicated, with the aid of educating our subscribers or followers, the whole thing from A to Z, so that his Home Business will be profitable, and he will make us greater productive through default. With the internet, humans can leverage on the Web to construct their enterprise at the remedy of their domestic and build desires of having extra time, cash, and freedom for themselves.

Benefit Of Working Online

Individuals who work online from home are always free to work anytime. They can make their schedule as per the demand.. Once the project is completed, they can take a break from work. Working online from home provide individuals calmness and happiness more when the work is completed. They feel no pressure since they are the boss.

Working online from home, they have an additional benefit, which is having all of their work-related items in one place. This saves time for arrangement since all the things are in one place.

Employees who work in an office every day are in a position where they experience traffic, transportation costs and other employees daily

Blog your Way to Internet Richness

The one thing about blogging that you have to know is that you can adapt it in a few unique manners. There isn't only one manner by which you can bring in cash out of a blog; there are a few. When you have your very own blog, it is a learning involvement with itself. In any case, simultaneously, the cash starts streaming in very quickly, which rouses you into draining your blog further.

An excellent stage to start your blog. You can write a blog anytime. You blog article should attract customers and relevant to your niche. Make readers visit your blog every day. You can share the latest updates on the blog.

Affiliate programs.

An affiliate application is virtually an application in which you earn commissions by using promoting anybody else's product or service. Alternatively, you can additionally earn cash with the aid of clear marketing for their site. If you pick out to be part of an affiliate application on the internet, it would be fine if you had your website, and ideally, one that is conducive to promoting the items and offerings of your service provider partner. In different words, it should be a website that caters to a precise crew of human beings or an area of interest market. If humans purchase your partner's merchandise thru your website, you will receive a share of the sale price.

Sell amazon product as an affiliate program

Clickbank Product as an affiliate

Work From Home Customer Service

It has usually been integral to making sure that as you discover work from a domestic job, you see that that without a doubt suit your wishes and is, in reality, what you would like it to be. Your perfect work at a domestic job has to be a job that you are already precise at, and one that you can without difficulty do from home. The humans who have the most success at work from domestic jobs can discover jobs that they already comprehend how to do or conditions that they are already doing, and flip them into exercise at local tasks. Therefore, if you are fascinated in work from domestic patron provider jobs, you already be aware of that you are going to have a proper shot at discovering appropriate employment. There are lots of motives that you will be in a position to locate desirable work from domestic client-provider jobs, and these motives consist of being in a place to sooner or later see the kind of work that you have been searching for, as correctly as

List of business ideas

- Social-Media Specialist

- Selling on eBay

- Home Bakery

- Graphic Design

- Personal Computer Training

- Home Tutoring

- Doggie Bed and Breakfast

- Music Teaching

- Virtual Assistant

- Web Design

- Sports Coaching and Training

- Makeup Consulting

- Research/Fact-Checking

- Video Service

- House Cleaning

- Bookkeeping

- Consultant on Foreign Cultures

- Cataloging Art Collections

- Soap and Lotion Making

- Scrapbooking

- Jewelry Making

- Furniture Making

- Antique Refurbishment

- Dog Walking

- Home Day Care

- Podcasting

- Car Resale

- Catering Service

- Party Planning

- Dance Instructor

- Music Teacher

- Party Planner

- Party Clown

- Dance Instructor

- YouTube Personality

- Jewelry Maker

- Personal Trainer

- Copywriter

- clothing Designer

- book Author

- Massage Therapist

- Hair Stylist

- Interior Designer

- Home Staging Business

- Seller of Collectibles

- Dog Groomer

- Pet Sitter

- Drone Trainer

- Personal Stylist

- Photographer

- Gift Basket Arranger

- Furniture Upcycler

- Bicycle Repair

- Baker

- Jam Seller

- Caterer

- Florist

- Fundraiser

- App Designer

- Landscape Designer

- Tie-dye Shirt Designer

- Life Coach

- Wedding Coordinator

- Henna Designer

- Glass Blower

- Publicist

- Vacation Rental Owner

- Mystery Shopper

- Yoga Instructor

- Travel Planner

- Bed and Breakfast Operator

- Christmas Tree Farmer

- Online Store

- Create an online store to s

- Virtual Assistant

- Build Passive Income with a Blog

- Become an Online Freelance Writer

- Start an Online Store

- Piece Together Some Micro Jobs

- Write and Publish an E-Book

- Surveys During Your Spare Time

- Join a Food Delivery Service

- Start a Catering Business

- Landscape Design

- Become a Tour Guide

- Start a DaycareIn Your Home

- Start an Elder Care Business

- Become a Dog Walker or Pet Sitter

- Travel Planning

- Start a House Cleaning Business

- Start a Voiceover Business

- Teach English to Overseas Students

- Start a Home Inspection Business

- Start a Massage Therapy Business

- Start a Tax Preparation Business

- Become a Hairstylist

- Start a Graphic Design Business

- Start a Bookkeeping Business

- Start a Copywriting Business

- Build a Translation Business

- Start a Grant Writing Business

- Do Medical Transcription from Home

- Collect Debt for a Living

- Create Homemade Goods for Etsy.com

- Start a Home-Based Organization Business

- Herb Farming

- Fix Broken Electronics

- Become a Tutor

- Become a Personal Trainer

- Teach Music Lessons

- Rent Out a Room in Your House

- Rent Out Your Car

- Invest In Real Estate

- Sell Your Stuff

- Invest in Stocks

- Start a Child Proofing Business

- Remove People's Junk

9 789354 381379